My Name is C. J. Starr & These R My Stories!
Vol. 1

C. J. Starr

My Name is C. J. Starr & These R My Stories! Vol. 1
Copyright © 2011 by C. J. Starr
ISBN: 978-1-892851-60-4

Cover by Night Owl Designs

Published by New Line Press

Printed in the United States of America

10 9 8 7 6 5 4 3 2 1

Dedicated to my good
friends, Valentine and April

Table of Contents

Five Delicious C. J. Starr Stories

Story 1: Housemates

Chapter One

Winter was closing down like a bankrupt mom and pop grocery store. Spring was about to hold its Grand Opening with a beautiful sixty degree temperature forecast. Yes... Winter had run its course. The snows had all melted and all of the Midwestern trees were laden with promising buds ready to unfold and display their varied hues of greenery. The renewal had begun.

Soon, robins would magically return from their southern climes and begin dancing around in little hops across suburban lawns and local parks where they'd noisily seek an early morning worm from their rapidly thawing mother earth.

Christy, short for Christina, woke at sunrise and wondered if she'd be able to sleep in, just a little longer, with all the spring peeping going on outside of her second story bedroom window. There wasn't any volume control for chirping birds, at least that she was aware of, and with that profound thought dancing through her head she decided to rise early and get the Christy Show off and on the road.

As Christy showered, she made mental notes on what she needed to do. Her lease was up and she had already turned in a formal notice to vacate her little one bedroom apartment. Amazing how things accumulate in just one year, she thought. This time, I'll get myself a walk-in closet, and then thought further, adding, with two bedrooms.

Lathering her blond hair, she envisioned her new, at home, office. She decided that she'd get a large desk and she'd have it set up to face a large window, one that would offer a pleasant view, maybe one that looked out onto a park or maybe even a forest.

Dreaming of the perfect apartment and oak desk led her into thoughts of William. Thoughts of how they had made love on his desk when they had worked overtime just after New Years. Thoughts of how scared she was of possibly getting caught, and yet how liberated she felt to be completely naked on top of his office desk.

Christy scooped a gob of the shampoo from her hair and brought it down between her legs where she covered her golden pussy hair with the gardenia scented bubbles and began a slow and gentle massage of her mound de Venus. The warmth of the pulsating water from a five-position showerhead and her beautiful thoughts of William's large penis sent her into a climatic moment of pure and un-adulterated ecstasy.

She laughed out loud, as she heard herself exclaim, "Oh God!" as a spasm of pleasure raced through her five-foot-five-and-a-half inch voluptuous frame.

Toweling with a thick luxurious towel, Christy dabbed herself dry before stepping on her bathroom scale. One-hundred and seven pounds the scale numerically announced. "Perfect!" she voiced aloud, and then took a quick survey of her petite body in the full-length mirror that paneled the bathroom door. She looked good. Damn good! And it made her happy that she kept her 25-year-old body in such excellent shape. The evening walks, all those hours at the gym; they were not wasted. Yes, she was fit and very, very attractive. Her self-confidence was solid and she knew that she was a gifted young woman who possessed one exceptionally desirable body.

Along with Christy's pretty face, complete with dimples when she smiled, came a bright 121 IQ that propelled her right through a Liberal Arts Degree at Vassar

College in Poughkeepsie, New York. And now, just three years out of college, she was promoted to Senior Vice Presidency at the Harris Bank in Chicago. The extra money she'd earn as a Senior V.P. would give her the large apartment and – the new convertible she had already picked out at the local BMW dealership. Life was good. Very good! And Christy thrived on it.

Chapter Two

At work by eight, after a ritual stop at Starbucks, Christy began the fun task of moving into her own private office. She'd now have a credenza behind her executive desk and -- a private secretary!

Oh, how sick is this, she beamed mentally. And when she sat down in the leather desk chair for the first time she felt a pleasure reminding her of that intense orgasm. And her thoughts raced to William and how badly she wanted him, physically, right there – in her office, on her desk - right then and there. And she laughed to herself, wondering if she was going on a psychological power trip.

Playfully, she pretended to hit the secretarial inter-com button and ordered William Barns into her office – IMMEDIATELY! And added, "And tell him to be fully erect when he gets here, please." Smiling for obvious reasons, she stood and went to her office door and looked out into the hall of desks where William would soon be sitting by eight-thirty, and she fixated on his desktop and envisioned once again the sexual romp they had excitedly shared there. It was such a wonderful madness, she, fondly so, recalled.

Entranced in thought, pondering her developing relationship, she was startled by John Hammer, Senior Vice President of commercial loans.

"Miss Rice? Missing your old desk already? I'll see if I can get it back for you, if you like?"

"Good Morning Mister Hammer. I see that you're in fine form this beautiful morning. Has one of the young tellers rebuked your sexual advances?"

"That's not funny, Christina. I want that Cannon file on my desk by nine, sharp. Or you will be back on the mortgage floor with your friend, Billy."

"You're so old school, Hammer. Why don't you lighten up and make this job enjoyable? The Cannon file is finished; I'll get it for you." Christy went into her new office and retrieved it from an orderly stack of transitional files she had set on her credenza.

Hammer followed her in, "The problem with you young women is sex. If it were up to me, we wouldn't have any females promoted beyond cashier. In a few months you'll quit and announce that you're pregnant or something and fifty accounts will suffer."

"You're nearing that fine line of sexual harassment, Mister Hammer."

Grabbing the file with a tinge of vehemence exuding from his action, Hammer walked briskly from her office, mumbling, but clearly stating, "Damn! A man can't say shit around here. What's the banking industry coming to?"

Christy shook her head in disbelief of his feminist bigotry. Hammer was known to run his banking affairs with an iron hand and the stories of his sexual escapades were legendary throughout the bank. The thing that really irked her was that so many of the women that worked for him would drop their panties in a two count if he were to even wink at them.

Hammer wasn't all that good looking, and his gruff manner was more like that of a high school disciplinary officer than a Senior Bank Vice President. Christy learned to keep his actions under a tight reign from day one.

The one story about him that Christina knew about, first-hand was at her first social function with Harris Bank. It was the Fourth of July and a large picnic was hosted by the company at a lakeshore park just off of the outer drive.

Hammer was caught red handed getting a blowjob by a young teller (the teller is now a branch manager in another state) and Christy was there and comforted the eighteen-year-old girl. The voluptuous red-head, known then as Red, was all apologetic and insisting that she was the cause of the naughty little interlude as she wiped his cum from her chest and halter top.

Hammer disappeared in the crowd, but was caught again, just two hours later, humping another guy's wife in the back of a Dodge custom van. Again, Christy happened to be there and saw the two scrambling to dress under the scowling eyes of her irate husband. The situation was somehow defused and Hammer went back to the beer kegs where he was openly bragging about the incident and boasting how he was in demand by all the women there at the picnic. The thing that appalled her was that he had a cheering-him-on audience of beer-filled employees.

Then, later, just before the fireworks began, Hammer approached her and offered Christy the use of his blanket to sit together and observe the pyrotechnic show. With an adamant refusal by her, Hammer continued his vagrant search looking for a willing blanket mate. Her recollection of that moment was that she was surprised he was able to stand as he staggered off quite drunk on his search for more sex.

Half way through the explosive sky display, Christy looked around to see if Hammer found a playmate to share his outdoor woolen bed. Sure enough, she saw him up on a small knoll with a large mound under the blanket right over his crotch. With a bright luminal burst from a firework, she perceived that the blanket had two feminine legs extended outward from the foot of the blanket. The bastard was getting yet another blowjob, as he observed the holiday final.

Then she recalled the first Christmas party she attended with the bank, the one that was held at the Continental Plaza. It was a formal dress party for the senior employees. She was the youngest employee there as a guest of Richard Smithe the bank President.

Hammer was there with his wife, an attractive brunette with huge boobs. Her cleavage went forward from a push up bra and her exposed flesh quivered like a Jell-O mold when she sipped on her glass of champagne. She complimented him in her looks and her stature. But, the two were never seen together for more than a minute or two as Hammer was always off flirting with every gown in the Plaza.

Right after the cordon bleu dinner, Hammer vanished. His wife, Caroline went from guest to guest asking if anyone had seen him. Christy felt bad for her, as she had personally seen him sneak out the door with a petite blonde that dressed more like an elf than a bank executive.

The elf and Hammer returned after an hour, or so. The elf's hair needed to visit a hairbrush and Hammer, well... Hammer needed his tuxedo ironed and he definitely needed to wipe the red lipstick off his neck. A lipstick shade that was easily matched to Santa's little helper.

Christy shook off her Hammer recollections and went out on the floor to finish moving the last few items from her old desk. As she passed William's cubicle she had a thought about her own actions there on the bank's highly polished piece of furniture.

With her office door left open, she watched the employees arrive and get ready for their nine a.m. opening. She was only looking for one employee in particular, William. When he finally entered and moved toward his open bay office, her heart did a small flip-flop with an emotional undertone. She was undeniably in love. And William Barns was the target of her affections. Christy deliberately left one folder in her old top drawer so that she'd have to walk back and pass his location. As soon as he had a minute to settle in, she moved out toward his cube.

"Good Morning Mister Barns. How are you this fine morning?"

"Hi Christy, you're being awfully formal this morning with the, Mister Barns? I guess that comes with your new territory. Should I call you Madam Vice President now?" and William laughed easily and not a bit intimidated with her new title and the hard-earned position that came with her new V.P. logo.

"No. No madam, please. I am a Ms. with no little 'r' in it, although, if someone is around, I would appreciate it if you would call me Ms. Rice. Just for fun. Okay?"

"Sure Christy, I mean – Ms. Rice." And they both laughed and they both understood that business was business. And that she'd only be Christy when they were alone.

"I'm going to go look at an apartment during my lunch break. Care to join me?"

"I'd love to! I break at 11:30 now, starting today -- since you moved up. Will that work?"

"Yes. I'm on a flexible lunch system now. Eleven-thirty it is, Mister Barns."

William looked around with deliberate caution, and then said, while winking, "Maybe we can swing by my place for a snack, Ms. Rice?"

Reddening ever so softly, Christina demurred with a, "We'll see, Mister Barns." And she left and returned to her office with a warm anticipatory smile that evoked her dimples, and a thought that gave her a warm sensation throughout her very being.

Chapter Three

At eleven-thirty sharp, Christy and William left the bank and headed north to view the apartment that she had made an appointment to see. It was a ten-minute drive and they found it easily with directions from a MapQuest. The apartment was on the third floor and had boasted a view of Lake Michigan. Something that wasn't visible when they pulled into the private parking lot.

The woman in the rental office, a forty something matron, took them up in the elevator and let them in. She left the key with Christy and excused herself; claiming that she was missing her eleven o'clock soap opera.

The apartment was perfect. It was spacious, had the required walk-in closet, carpeted in an earth-tone beige, a darling double sink bathroom, and a larger than expected (all oak) kitchen with a dining nook. The bedrooms both faced the lake as advertised and a sailboat was gracefully heeling just off the shore. The downward view was a tree-lined street and no other buildings blocked her view. Her heart was pounding with anticipation. She was sold. This would be Christina's castle – if she could afford it?

"How much is the rent?" William asked, "I bet it's exuberant...but just look at that view!"

"It's fabulous, isn't it?"

"Yeah, how much is it, Chris?"

"I don't know yet. There wasn't a price listed in the paper. Come on. Let's go down and find out."

Bill took her in his arms and gave her a loving squeeze and then they kissed, longer than they both had realized. Yes, and if they had kissed any longer, it would have counted as an act of commingling.

Christy pulled away and said, "Later for this, Bill. Lunch is passing too quickly. I need to find out what this will cost me. Let's go."

The sticker shock hit Christy right between the eyes. She had a brief moment of vertigo as the soap opera addict casually stated, "Seventeen-hundred a month, first and last months rent, up front...plus a five hundred dollar non-refundable cleaning deposit."

"Oh my," Christina stammered out. "Does that in-clude the utilities?"

"It includes the gas, garbage, and a covered parking spot; the tenants pay their own electric."

"The ad said there was a pool. How do I get to that?"

"Down the hall, last door on the right. Your apartment key opens the door. The pool doesn't open until the first of June. But there's talk of opening it earlier this year. The hot tub is opened all year."

"Oh, I didn't know there was a hot tub."

"Yes. There isn't a laundry room. There are laundry hookups in all the apartments. Did you see them?"

"No. I didn't."

"They're in the kitchen away from everything. Most women see them right away. Some don't."

"Come on William, let's take a quick look at the pool."

Hand in hand, the lovers walked around the pool and even turned on the hot tub jets before returning the apartment key back to Sharon, the soap-a-holic, "I'll call with my decision this afternoon. Have you had many lookers?"

"You were the first, dear. But it only went up yesterday. Do you want to put down a deposit? They don't last long in this location."

"We really have to run. We're on our lunch hour. I'll call you when we get back to the office. But I think I can swing it." Christina gave Sharon one of her new V.P.

business cards, and then pleaded, "Don't rent it before you hear from me, Okay?"

Sharon looked at the card and had to squint as she read it. "Will you two be moving in together?"

"No," Christy demurred, with a smile in her voice. "For right now, it's just me."

Chapter Four

Christina signed a one-year lease that very evening. Her dream apartment was now a reality. Although, the BMW was now placed in her limbo of wants. But, after all, when all was said and done, there wasn't a thing wrong with her five-year-old, paid-for, Chevy Nova.

William was with her when she paid the rent and received her key. In the elevator, they kissed and Bill pointed out to her his full erection as the door opened out onto the third floor-carpeted hallway.

Once inside of Christina's new digs, Christy acknowledged his growing passion and playfully unzipped his pants. Then, helping her remove her business dress, the two were soon rolling around the floor naked with their bank attire littering the alcove leading into her expansive living room.

"Hold it. Hold it!" exclaimed Christy, "I've got to turn up the heat, Ice Boy. It's freezing in here."

Bill rolled onto his back and let her up, marveling at her beautiful body and the way her breast swayed as she stood, "You've got a perfect body, Ms. Rice."

"And this perfect body wants that erection of yours inside of me, Mister Burns...as soon as I find the damn thermostat."

Bill sat up awaiting her return, "I'll need to make sure you're wet enough, so hurry it up, cutie. My tongue awaits you."

Upon her return, she straddled his face as he licked around her inner thighs. Then, as he stuck his tongue between her pussy lips and touched her clitoris with a soft darting action, she grabbed his hair and pulled him full flush and into her moistening pussy, "Oh William!" was the only words she could express as her demanding need of sexual release increased.

William felt the spasm of orgasm overtake her body as she pressed her pelvis hard against his lips. With a firm grasp on her ass, he assisted her frantic grind into his face and forced his tongue as deep as he could into her vagina's juicy orifice.

"Oh my God!" she screamed as her body tightened around his loving and most active mouth. Then, the full moment of ecstasy arrived and the one passionate word, "William!" shot from the depths of her pleasure-center as orgasmatic needles overwhelmed her every sense. If there were a neighbor home during this primeval release, surely one would have come to investigate the actions of this William that screamed out to the whole and entire universe at large...

William helped her to sit beside himself where he cuddled her still trembling torso in his strong arms. Her heart was a snare drum pounding out delight in a quickened pulse of pure and uncontrollable lust.

"Oh William." she cooed while locked in his gentle embrace, "That was just...too, too fantastic!"

William, still erect and hard as an ingot of steel, asked her in a soft whisper, "May I enter you my love?"

With a broad, dimpled smile and a warm want of him inside of her, Christy moved out from his warm arms and spread herself out on the deep pile carpeting spreading her legs sexually open in an inviting want of his beautiful penis.

William entered her slow and ever so gentle; and then, with her fluids naturally lubricating his drive, he increased his pace to a maddening frenzy of in and out strokes that brought Christina's need back into the limelight of their openly shared state of sexual giving.

When she felt him nearing his deserved fulfillment she tightened in on her vagina muscles and let her own senses join in with his need to ejaculate and visit the world of his most ecstatic pleasure. She too, found herself entering that world of oneness with all of heaven's wonderful mysteries as she experienced a second orgasm – simultaneously, with her most cherished friend and lover, William (Bad Boy) Barns.

Chapter Five

After showering in the nakedness of the apartment (There wasn't even a shower curtain in the glistening white bathtub), they dried off with William's boxer shorts. They then dressed and moved from room to room as Christy planned her move-in that would commence on the very next morning.

Her biggest excitement was her future office. It would remain bare until she could get the large desk delivered; except for a few boxes of her books.

William shared her enthusiasm and listened intently as she described her dream décor right down to the color of the push-pins she'd use on her soon to be hung cork board, the position of a yet-to-be purchased hanging fern, and the black-out curtains that she'd hang so that she could work naked, "...without any seagulls looking in on me," it was a statement that made them both laugh, an easy laugh that only an intimate couple could share, hooting at the pure idiocy of her illogical reasoning. Peeping seagulls!

They stopped for Chinese take-out on Randolph Street and ate at Christina's. William helped her with the last minute packing which took them until two in the morning. The mover's would arrive at seven, and everything was now ready for them -- except her bed.

"We're down to the bed. Do you want to take it apart now...or sleep on it?" Bill questioned.

"I'm ready to sleep. How about you? My back is killing me. You'll have to rub my back. Let's go." Christy led William into the bedroom, "You're staying here tonight, like it or not."

"I like it. Did you leave out your massage oil?"

"No. All packed. But you still have to rub my back. I can do without the oil," she cooed, as she turned off the light, "I did leave out a couple of towels..."

"That's what I like about dating a Vice President. They're always one step ahead of you."

Christina plopped down on messy bed fully clothed, "You'll have to undress me, Willy. I'm just too tired. Would you mind?"

With a hint of laughter and sincere note of playfulness, Willy, stripped off his clothes while saying, "Mind?

Hell no, Ms. Pres," and with the hands of a magician, had her naked and reaching for a pillow to rest her head.

Bill knelt down between her spread out legs and began a series of firm strokes with his hands from the small of her back on up to her shoulders. Her flesh was so soft and silky that it excited him to full erection by the time he made the fourth sweep down alongside of her backbone. A delightful throb came forth from his crotch as he let his fingertips slide curiously down her well-contoured rump. Stopping his play at her butt dimples, he smoothed the flesh outward from their center and marveled at how they resumed their form when he released the slight pressure he had exerted.

Bill scooted backward a few inches and bent forward allowing his penis head to swipe across her the cheeks of her ass. This move caused more pangs of desire to shoot up from his testicles and elicited an, "Oh my!" from the prostate, and now fully relaxed, Christy.

"Oh, you like that, eh?" came back Willy's whispered response, "Do you want to take it up your ass?"

"No. No up the ass, not tonight, you're doing just fine with the massage."

Bill continued his long strokes up to the nape of neck and every time he touched her hairline, his erection would probe a shallow dip between her mounded cheeks. The pleasure he was deriving from this poking effort was a totally new sensation and made his mental excitement grow to a near orgasmatic need. His mind went kinky as he envisioned entering her from behind after an application of petroleum gel about her tightened and verbally forbidden orifice.

With his foreplay, his own mental foreplay heightening to near ejaculation, Christy found her own sensations and needs cultivating wildly inside her mind. She abruptly squiggled around and moved to a halfway sitting position, "I need to see what's going on back here," as she eyed his bulbous-headed erection.

In the darkened room, she had to move closer to his penis that he was now grasping in his hand, "Oh Bill!"

Christy twisted herself around, "Let me help you with that," and she took, little Bill, from his grasp and began a soft up-and-down massage of his huge and anvil hard erection that included his tightened scrotum encasing his most assuredly sensitive balls.

Christy felt a drop of sperm escaping his puffed and warm penis head. In a fiery move of uninhibited desire to enthrall her own mounting passion, she took him full into her mouth and began a soft suck to extract his saline tasting premature ooze. The taste of his love juice bolstered her sucking action and forced Bill to use every mental restraint in his body to keep from exploding into her mouth.

Christy knew he was withholding and countered with a feathery move of her free hand across the swollen pouch at the base of his penis. This small swipe elicited a moan of abject pleasure from the sexual depths of Willy's very being, "Oh! Fuck. I'm entering orgasm, Christy!" he blared out in an attempted whisper of his uncontrollable intention.

Christy knew she had him. She wanted the warmth of his orgasm to spew into her mouth and fill her pallet with that gift of euphoric ejaculate. She grasped his balls and gave them a gentle downward tug of passion war.

In a beautiful moment of supreme release, Christy's mouth filled with the hot release of his total essence of being a man. It was a massive explosion of pure adulterated sperm and the wonderment of orgasm so powerfully loosened sent her groping for her clitoris that needed only the slightest touch to send her very self into a marvelous swoon of homogenized carnal eruption that encapsulated her very soul.

The tender hug and soft after play of their mutual and sensuous touching put them both in a state of nirvana; a euphoric oneness took over their hearts and the beauty of a needed sleep sent them both into the nether world of pure rest and un-demanded life rejuvenation. And they slept... Entwined souls of love, enjoying a peace that only true lovers ever get to know.

Epilogue:

The movers were on time. Everything arrived intact at Christy's new digs. By sunset, the furniture was all set up and arranged to Christy's content.

Pizza was delivered by seven.

At eight, Christy and William were showered (and had all of the towels exposed for use) and had just crawled into Christy's freshly made bed. Their anticipations, her for another needed massage, and him for an anticipated repeat of that morning's escapades, were solid fixtures within their individual minds. And -- it would soon be so, too!

Christy had just taken little Bill full into her mouth when the building's intercom sounded announcing a visitor in the lobby. Scrambling for her robe, leaving Bill hanging, she dashed wildly to the call box, "Who is it?" she pleaded.

Security responded, "It's a man named Hammer. Should I send him up?"

"Hammer?! She exclaimed, with a contorted look on her face, "Ask him what he wants, please." Christy found herself stammering this out in a total state of bewilderment.

After a brief pause, security announced, "He has a magnum of Champagne... He wants to know (Christy could hear Hammer laughing in the back-ground) if you'd like to be housemates tonight?"

The End!

STORY 2: NOWHERE TO TURN

LENORA'S DAY OFF

It was mid August in the upscale suburbs of North Chicago. Lake Michigan modified the stagnant warm air enveloping the city proper and made the close-to-shore homes comfortable without air-conditioning. Lenora Moore looked at the two-foot ceramic-backed thermometer behind the pool's diving board and smiled as she read the 77-degree mark. It was a perfect day to sun and lounge quietly as she finished reading her erotic Harlequin romance novel that was totally making her horny.

The dark haired, brown-eyed beauty was twenty-nine, and had a body that was a solid ten on any man, or women's scorecard. She kept it toned and healthy at Bally's gym where she worked out on a regular basis. Lenora and her husband Robert played competitive tennis on the weekends and ran in marathons whenever they got the chance.

Robert, or as she sometimes called him, Bob, was as far as she knew, a stock broker, but he more precisely referred to himself as the most aggressive investment banker in all of the Chicago Megalopolis.

Lenora loved her job as a graphic artist with Chicago's Art Institute. What had started out as a hobby, turned into a job, and that job turned into a career, one that she was completely enthralled to have. Together, their incomes allowed them financial freedom from any and all of life's little mundane needs. By all accounts, they are a couple just like out of one of the romance novels Lenora liked to read.

But this narrator hears Lenora calling, and shall let her take over the story from here:

Lenora's Blackberry played out, "Dancing Queen" from the musical, Mamma Mia, as she read the last sentence of chapter twelve. "Lenora here," she answered with a lilt in her voice, and started to ask, "How may I help you?" She then caught herself, cleared her throat and said, "Hello?"

"Hey sweetie, I only have a second," Bob spoke rapidly, "I'm going up the Hancock for a business dinner. I won't be in until late. Don't wait up for me, I'll be drinking a little and will want to get some sleep. Kiss! Kiss!" And the Blackberry disconnected. It figures. I get the day off and Bob has to work late. Oh well. That's life in the big city. She always wanted to be a city girl like the women in Sex in the

City, she saw herself as a "Charlotte" type, but somehow her life wasn't as glamorous as the fictional characters as the Sex and the City girls.

Setting down her novel, she went to the edge of the pool and with a pedicure toenail, tested the water. She sat down and lowered her slim legs into the water, thinking, this is the second night this week that Bob has had a dinner engagement for his office. And she thought further as she kicked water into the air with her feet; he was out twice last week, too. And with that recollection, a pang of jealousy gripped her deep in her chest and her feet suddenly became idle and the pool water became very still and calm, very unlike the steam that was rising inside of her.

She decided food would help, so still dripping, she went into the kitchen and made herself a deviled egg sandwich. As she ate, she recalled her earlier plan to seduce Robert when he came home from work. She was going to make him his favorite dish, Chicken Kiev, with a chilled bottle of Merlot breathing, invitingly, on the center of a candle-lit table. Robert loved his wine, and it always became a trigger to their sexual playfulness.

She had a new Victoria's Secret matching sexy number, too. But now, she'd have to wait to show it off to him. Her thoughts wandered relentlessly on her earlier, loving plan, right down to the fresh cut flowers, which actually for her, not Robert. Lenora knew what Bob liked. She knew she could draw out his pleasure and maximize him until she was ready, and how she would wantonly beg him to enter her. Then, she wondered, only momentarily, if all men were so easy to control by such simple playfulness. She put her plate into the Bosch stainless steel dishwasher, retrieved a bottle of ice-cold Evian water and went back outside to her thoughts and her book.

Blake, the seventeen-year-old hunk next door, was out in his driveway shooting baskets beyond the privacy fence. Lenora could see the ball arch up and hit the net, but she couldn't actually see him. He'd dribble a few times and then shoot. She didn't like the noise. It distracted her from reading. But Blake was always courteous to her, though Robert didn't seem to like him much, but to her, he always seemed to pay extra attention, he was always smiling, always willing to do odd jobs for her here and there.

Lenora watched the orange ball hit the rim and bounce toward fence. It hit the top of the redwood and bounced onto the pool skirt where it rolled past her lounge chair and came to rest in her flowerbed. "I got it Blake!" she yelled out. She got up and went for the ball. As she bent down to pick it up, Lenora became self-conscious of her thong bathing suit, and hoped Blake wasn't watching over the latticework. As she stood, she heard Blake's deep voice. "Hello. Mrs. Moore. Sorry about the ball. I'll try keeping it in our yard. Great day for a swim isn't it? Nice suit," he blurted out, and then blushed.

Lenora knew full well that her ass was exposed to the smiling teenager. "You don't need to blush Blake. Sex is a natural part of life, and I'm sure you've seen lots of naked asses as handsome as you are."

"Well -- I…" Blake started to stutter. "I do see lots of thongs along the beach."

"I'm sure that you do, Blake." She smiled openly and tossed the ball back to him. "Just try keeping your balls to yourself," she laughed.

Blake couldn't help but turn his efforts from her firm ass to her equally beautiful breasts. He knew her husband was away a lot and wondered if Mr. Moore fully appreciated the piece of art he had in his wife.

Without trying to conceal his efforts, he tried to make conversation, "Is that what they call a postage-stamp bikini top?"

"Yes, Blake… And you can stop staring now and get back to shooting hoops."

"Thanks for the ball. I'll be going now." He turned and dribbled off and out the gate closing it softly behind him. The future, No. 34, Bulls wannabe continued swishing the net and palm dribbling around his driveway, another five minutes and then silence reclaimed the neighborhood.

Lenora picked up her book and began reading Chapter 13, "Travis, my darling. It's been a long time since a man held me in his arms as caring as you do. Let's leave this farm town and move to the city. You could find work in one of the factories up north and..." Lenora set the book down, sensing Blake's eyes upon her.

"Blake?" she called out toward the redwood fence, "What are you doing?"

"Sorry Mrs. Moore."

"Blake, how many times have I told you – it's Lenora. Mrs. Moore makes me feel so old!"

"Okay, Lenora." Just watching her gave him a hard-on. He made a fast exit up to the privacy of his bathroom.

Lenora smiled to herself. She had suspected that Blake had snuck a peek at her through the fence on more than one occasion. She didn't mind, it made her feel sexy. She was nearing that dreadful age of thirty and she couldn't stand the thought of being over the hill.

Shaking from her head the horrific thought of getting older, she removed her bathing suit and fully naked, slid freely into the pool wondering if hunk Blake was still around – and watching. As she stroked around the refreshing and soothing water of the pool, with each lap she took, she fantasized what it would be like to slam-dunk the ball-playing hunk next door.

ROBERT IS SO BUSTED!

Lenora rapidly read four more chapters. Travis is one hell of a lover, she thought, as she dog-eared the beginning of chapter 17. She was tempted to skip ahead to the last page to see what would happen, but decided to finish the book when she'd go to bed, alone, later that night.

She walked to her bedroom and placed the book on her nightstand. She carefully placed her bathing suit on a towel rack to dry. It was in her mind to take a late dip if Basketball Jones decided to shoot some late night hoops, which was something that he did quite often. Though she may just go sans the suit.

Looking in the full-length mirror, she was pleased with the sight of her toned body. Right down to her pelvic hair that she had carefully had waxed into the shape of a heart.

Robert wondered about her sanity (jokingly, of course) when she did that and told her so, and he shook his head when she seemed surprised by his unenthusiastic response. "What was next," he wondered, "a tattoo?"

But, it was for him that she had the heart made – it was an artistic expression of how she felt about him. She thought it quite brilliant and original. And now, it was only herself that enjoyed it. She lightly stroked the fine hair and it was enough to get her juices flowing.

A tingling sensation enveloped Lenora, right down to her artsy heart. She moved to the bed and sprawled out on top of her goose down comforter. The fabric was cool on her nudity and felt extremely pleasant. She rolled around the king size bed letting the soft bedding embrace her flesh and further titillate her aroused state.

Scooting herself to the bed's edge she opened the top drawer of the nightstand and reached for Big Bobby. Big Bobby was a large dildo that Robert had given her upon his return from one of his many business trips to Vegas. He said it was something to keep her company while he was away. She always wondered about why he insisted on going on business trips alone, but he said she was just whining about nothing, so she didn't question it, and she had her work, so it just became a part of their lifestyle.

She turned Big Bobby on, as the desire for an orgasm was the only thought present in her mind at that moment. Rolling onto her back, she began a slow massage of her brunette artistry nested between her luscious legs. Big Bobby performed better than most of the men Lenora had ever known, especially when she turned it up to level four; the max.

After her routine orgasm, she took a shower and soaped herself luxuriously, and it was then that Lenora began to contemplate Robert's recent neglect of her personal wants. It had been weeks since he had given her oral gratification. Actually, it had been closer to a month. His late nights at work, and his business dinners were becoming more and more frequent. She had called him on his absences but he told her that she was being "paranoid" and "crazy." And so she set her suspicions aside.

But her doubts were becoming louder and louder in her trusting mind. She recalled how her father had had affairs on her mother, how their relationship ended in a bitter divorce. She painfully remembered how it all came to light after her father frequently started staying away from home – just like Robert was doing now. And then it dawned on her. There was a pattern and it was repeating itself with her husband, with her beloved Robert. That asshole! She had a moment of classical eureka! Oh my God! She thought. And then, out loud and to the entire universe, she screamed, "He's having an affair!"

Lenora toweled herself dry with fear. Her mind raced over the last several weeks. No flowers, no chocolates, no intensity with their lovemaking. As she thought

about it, their sex life had fizzled out. Thinking about it
further, it pissed her off that he had bought her the massag-
er. At first, she'd thought it was something to add to their
sex play, but now she was getting angry. He was sending her
a message in a bottle, or rather, a sex message via a rubber
penis, and it pissed her off.

   Things started to fall into place in her mind; the late
nights, the drop off in their sex life, the far-a-away look he
got whenever she mentioned starting a family. How many
times she'd caught him in a lie yet he always brushed them
off with his convincing yet pathetic excuses. And she
believed him.

   She tried to remember where he said he was going
for dinner, but her thoughts were a frenzy of every lie he
ever told her. Then she remembered, the John Hancock.
She tore through her closet looking for the right dress.
Opting for a black number that gave her courage and
showed off her cleavage, she dressed in a hurry and ma-
naged to get her makeup on in less than a two count.

   She studied herself in the mirror and knew that she
was a dynamite vixen, she had a natural, innate beauty and
she knew it. She hunted for a small clutch and wished she
had a handgun to put into it. Instead, she opted for the Big
Bobby dildo, and stuffed it into her purse thinking at the
very least she'd wack Robert over the head with it.

   By the time she arrived at the Hancock building, she
had calmed down on the drive into the Loop, but after she

tossed the keys to the valet and found herself going up the elevator, she started to shake. She had no script in mind for what she might say when she found Robert.

Turning more than a few heads with her stunning looks, she searched the tables on the 95th floor and the world famous Signature Room.

She asked the hostess about dinner reservations for Robert Moore.

"Are you with the party?"

The suspicion meter in Lenora's brain was on fire. "No. I mean, yes." She didn't know what she meant. Her brain was melting and she felt as if she could barely breathe.

"Well, what is it? Yes or no?"

"I'm his wife," She blurted out. Her voice was quivering. She reached into her purse and pulled out a twenty. "Just tell me where he's at." She was in a hurry and had no time for small talk; she wanted to see what the hell he was up to. Robert told her he was going to a business dinner, and she was almost afraid to find out the truth.

The hostess nonchalantly took the cash. "He's not in the restaurant down here, he's up in The Signature Lounge, on the 96th floor," adding under her breath, "…at a table for two."

The words reverberated in Lenora's mind.

"Do you know how to get there?" The hostess asked.

"I can find it!" Lenora could feel her heart breaking and wished she would have taken a Valium. It had to be a business dinner. He wouldn't lie to her. Perhaps she was crazy and paranoid as he often accused her. But at least this way, she'd know the truth and she could get back home and snuggle back into her bed knowing she was not insane.

She headed to the 96th floor to the equally world class Signature Lounge where the city lights supposedly glimmered in the night sky (according to the sign in the elevator).

Lenora's worst fears were confirmed as she saw Robert with a blonde woman who was clearly more than a business associate by their blatant actions in the lounge. "Are you fucking kidding me," she said under her breath. That fucking asshole! "And with this bimbo?" And that was the best he could do? He was fucking around on her with some bleached-blonde who looked like a whore from Wells Street, the local hooker shopping mall. Robert had no clue Lenora was watching, as he leaned over and kissed the woman full on her lips.

Lenora wondered how he would explain his way out of that full-on lip lock with Miss Tits?

Lenora's eyes fixated on the bitch wearing a cliché clinging red dress and -- was that a tattoo on her shoulder?

Robert's hand was under the table and up the dress of his latest lover. He was in heaven. His fingers were feeling her moist vagina, and his tongue was deep into her mouth. Later his tongue would be deep between the barrier of her labia and inside her never-ending access that she gave him. She made love to him in ways that his wife never did, or would ever dare. His wife didn't play the game. Not like this woman did. This woman wasn't offended by Robert's desire to be tied up, it was mere sex play, and together they played a lot. She was sexually open to have sex play with more than a dildo.

Robert and the woman ignored the stares coming their way. He was a player in the city and he could do what he wanted – where he wanted. Money bought you freedom, he'd learned early in his life, and it was money that was buying him this evening and one fabulous fuck later.

Their tongue exchange was interrupted by a flying dildo that landing smack in the center of the table, knocking over their drinks and sending the crystal glasses crashing onto the floor.

The blonde slut didn't seem fazed in the slightest. Almost as if being confronted by a wife was an everyday occurrence.

Standing up, Robert stared face to face with his fuming wife. He calmly asked, "Darling, what are you doing here?"

C. J. Starr

THE IMMEDIATE AFTERMATH

Lenora's heart was beating faster then the wings of a hungry hummingbird sucking nectar from a honeysuckle bush. Her makeup smeared as her tears made her look like a rabid zombie as she ran from the lounge to the comfort of the 96th floor Signature ladies room.

She sobbed at the marble counter in the bathroom, and thoughts of jumping from the roof of the Hancock filled her stressed soul. She was a loyal wife, a faithful, loving, caring wife. She played the role and in the short time they'd been married, he's already cheating on her? "What the fuck happened?" She said in a loud and upset voice.

Before she knew it, she found herself on the cold floor, hearing her own sobs echoing and she didn't know how to stop the flow of tears. She started to stand but gave it up as her legs were shaking awkwardly from an inner rage. She had lost control. She was so angry she wanted to kill him. But she had to get up off the floor first.

And then suddenly she felt a shift inside. The tear parade ended. She took in a deep breath and exhaled slowly with sure and deliberate control. Her temporary insanity had given away to an open awareness of what had just transpired.

Still on the floor, she tried to calm her breathing, and let her mind fill with the moment. Her marriage was over. She thought about this a second and concluded that it wasn't all that great a marriage after all.

A stall door opened and a woman wearing a print suit and a huge white purse exited and approached Lenora.

"Are you okay, honey?" asked the bleached-blonde woman. Lenora guessed her to be about fifty but with Botox who the hell could tell age anymore.

The woman with the tight face reached down to help Lenora up from the hard marble floor.

"I'm fine."

"Well, if you don't mind me saying so, you don't look so great."

"Let me rephrase this then," Lenora said. "I'm as fine as a woman can be who has just caught her cheating bastard of a husband with another woman." With her voice returning to a near normal tone, adding, "My marriage is over."

With the words, "My marriage is over" out in the air for the universe to absorb, Lenora felt herself start to shake again. The stranger, who for some reason had taken a sudden interest in Lenora pulled her into an embrace, "Sweetie, it's going to be okay."

"No, no it's not!" Lenora said as she pulled away from the aged bimbo. She didn't know who this woman in the bathroom was, but she didn't need her patronizing her or offending hug. "I'll be fine," Lenora said. "Thanks for your help." Lenora immediately felt guilty for being rude. Here this woman was trying to be kind and she was being a bitch. It made her feel like she was playing a part in a bad movie and had to adlib every line of a super bad role, she was felt dazed and confused, and wanted a director to yell, cut!

Lenora got up and went over to the basin and splashed cold water on her face. The woman followed her.

"That's a good idea. Get washed up, settle down, and then if you feel like it, I've been known to be a great listener." The woman handed Lenora a hand towel. "You can tell me all about it."

Lenora had the urge to run back into the restaurant and have it out with Robert but instead found herself agreeing to the offer from a stranger. With her head nestled against her broad shoulder, Lenora felt comforted. She hadn't felt that comforted in a long time. For some reason this stranger, this woman she just met in the restroom made her feel as her world wasn't crashing down around her. She made her feel important enough to have taken an interest in her, which at first annoyed the hell out of Lenora but when she thought about it, it was the kind of thing someone back home would do – go out of their way for someone in need, not necessarily something she'd found in the city.

Reaching out her hand to Lenora, the woman smiled, "Come with me dear heart. I know the perfect place where we can sit and just talk."

NO TURNING BACK

The heat outside was oppressive as the women walked to an office building on Michigan Avenue. During the short walk, Lenora learned that the woman was Nancy Farmington, that she's an Estates Attorney, and that she'd been divorced three times, vowing never to remarry.

Nancy's office bespoke of wealth and abstract comforts that most mere mortals only dream about. It was huge and designed for the ease of entertaining Nancy's clients. A Rubin was hung with casual lighting behind her seven foot uncluttered desk. The couches and chairs matched the carpeting, but they were all leather and as soft as a crust-less loaf of bread.

Nancy led Lenora past all the fluff and they went deep into her inner sanctum. Beyond the fifteen-foot conference table and matching captain chairs was a cozy little hidden room. It was an inner home, complete with what Nancy laughingly called a "napping bed." There was a bar cart, small refrigerator, and a full bathroom, one that sported gold faucets and an inlaid glass mosaic power shower. The secret room was an impressive nook by any standard of wealth that could be individually personified.

"Sit here," Nancy instructed in a firm voice. And Lenora sat, still trying to take in the grand opulence of her surroundings.

With a lilt in her voice, "This is beautiful, Nancy. It must have cost you a small fortune."

"It's a business expense. I work extreme hours and I need this room to rest from time to time."

Nancy went to the liquor wagon where she began making a pair of powerful rum drinks. She prided herself on making them to perfection, and kept a healthy supply of fresh fruits that were needed and she had them replenished daily. It was her life's passion to make them. She had learned this delicate chore when she lived with her parents briefly on the enchanted island of Jamaica.

Setting out the sweetly garnished drinks, Nancy sat easily down next to Lenora who was slightly facing her, "Okay, my new friend...let's talk. Start at the beginning."

Lenora reached her drink and took a deep gulp of what would soon turn into her third direly needed non-medicinal tranquilizer. As the story unfolded in an open and unabashed narration, Nancy listened with the depth and intensity of the old master, Freud incarnated. After Lenora's third drink the saga of her misery was out on the table of emotional heartaches.

Lenora, now sipping on her fourth floral arrangement, began to laugh at her own damnable situation, and began relating the desire she felt for her seventeen-year-old neighbor, "I bet he doesn't even have pubic hair yet." She giggled, and never paid any attention to Nancy's knee brushing deliberately but ever so deftly up against her own. And...Lenora didn't think twice when Nancy asked to see the heart shaped tuft of hair that she had noticed while her dress was rumpled upward as she lay weeping on the ladies room floor.

Lenora, dizzy from the 150 proof rum, quickly stood, hiked up her dress hem, and exposed her panty-less virginal artwork.

"Oh!" exclaimed Nancy, "That is simply exquisite, Len," and then asked, "I must feel it! Would you mind, dear?"

Lenora was the proverbial, "Three sheets to the wind" and with a small quick hic-up even spread her legs ever so slightly for Nancy's hand to have clean access to brush over her delicate art work.

With a clinical tone in her voice, Nancy demurred, "My God, Lenora. That's the nicest thing I ever felt in my whole entire life." And her voice lowered an octave and she mused with a charming request, "I must look a little closer. Do you mind?"

"Do I Mind? No. I don't mind at all. As a matter of fact – hic – It feels damn fantastic! But I am getting just a little bit embarrassed... But..." and then she laughed; which came out more like an insane giggle of naughtiness.

Nancy wasted no time to investigate the obviously high but willing brunette's private domain. With a practiced effort, Nan titillated every sexually sensitive hair that resided between Lenora's shapely legs.

"Oh Nancy!" cried out Lenora as she squeezed her legs together entrapping her host's most talented fingers, "Did you learn this down in Jamaica, too! Hic..."

Nancy dimmed the lights. She started up some soothing music with the push of a button on a remote and led Lenora happily over to the executive napping bed where she guided her down to a horizontal position, "Just relax here, my pet. I'm going to massage away some of that angst you've built up." She directed Lenora to lie on her back and she was instantly enveloped into the fluffy, silk covered bedding.

Helping Lenora escape the confines of her dress was an easy task for the formidable seductress, Nancy. The rum was laced with a Jamaican aphrodisiac called loboci-duce, which is made from a Cuban palm frond extract. Soon, Lenora would have an overwhelming desire to suckle clitorises, and Nancy was just throbbing inside for this oral need to kick in on her luscious, luscious prey.

To keep Lenora awake, Nancy urged her to talk about recent nice things going on in her life as she stroked her hand all about her subtle breasts and abdomen.

"I think I'd like to make love with my neighbor's kid, Blake. I know I gave him an erection today. I saw it rise tight in his shorts. And I really wanted to pull it out and go down on him. Suck him until..." Lenora stopped in mid sentence and looked over at Nan's crotch.

"Go on, Lenora," cooed Nancy. "Suck him until, what?"

Lenora reached her hand toward Nancy's dress in an effort to pull it up, to expose her... Her desire to lick, slurp, and suck on her pussy was overwhelming. Good lord, Lenora thought, what had happened to her? She wasn't a lesbian, she'd never been with a woman, yet she had this overwhelming urge to suck her dry.

Nancy stood and shed her dress and quickly stepped out of her crotch-less panties. Her own orgasmic need and anticipation were growing wildly and near the limit of crossing over into the state of abject uncontrollability.

The passion serum was beginning to activate Lenora's needs. Lenora's mouth began to salivate and clitoral visions, beautiful, desirous visions danced vividly through her mind. She wanted Nancy's muff flush on her mouth, flush to her lips – so flush that her tongue could lap out and contact her damp clitoris.

Nancy knew the sexual power-drug was there and now openly activated. She placed her left leg up on the mattress and exposed her light fine-haired pussy a mere two feet from Lenora's tongue-moistened lips.

Nancy's thumb entered Lenora's vulva moisture just at the moment Lenora's face impacted with Nancy's offered fare. Frenzy ensued, a sucking and tonguing of utter madness and totally absorbing both of them in their climax seeking needs. Nancy ground her hips wildly into Lenora's lust to suck and lick and...

Nancy entered orgasm as Lenora's legs clamped down on her manipulative hand, a hand that was now full inside of Lenora's vagina performing a full twisting fist fuck. The sounds of pleasure filled the room in a duet of satisfaction yelps and cries to their majestic creators. Multiple expletives were openly and uncontrollably exhorted along with the throbs of extended orgasm and secondary eruptions of latent carnal pleasure.

The two women breathed like they had just finished a 10K run along the Lakeshore. Both spent, both relieved of mounted desires, one for pure pleasure and one from a drug induced need.

Nancy stood by her panting victim who was incoherently mumbling for more in a sad pleading of induced want to please.

Catching her breath, but still not fully satiated, Nancy ran her hands over the still throbbing flesh of Lenora and spoke, "You like this so much, my dear. I'm going to give you more. Lie back my precious, lie back." And Lenora did. And Nancy climbed onto the bed and straddled Lenora's self-moistened mouth and giggled freely as Lenora's tongue danced in and out and all about her now tender to the touch pleasure points.

Lenora engulfed the clitoral mound and sucked hard and determined on Nancy's juiced up needs. Throbs of sick joy pulsated throughout Nancy's body and soul. Orgasms were coming so fast and sure that they were no longer being counted and the muted screams became almost continuous as the sucking chaos continued for well over an hour before Lenora just stopped and went into a non-responsive snore that accompanied her pass out.

Nancy spent a few minutes fondling Lenora's breast. She then rolled her over and massaged her ass kneading the soft flesh with still desirous touches from her manicured fingers. The manic session was over. Naked except for her pearls, Lenora was left alone atop the bedding as Nancy stepped into the kaleidoscopic paneled executive shower.

THE PLOT THICKENS

Nancy returned naked, except for a towel wrapped around her wet hair, and checked on Lenora. She pulled a cover up over her peacefully asleep body with a genuine concern for her comfort. She looked at Lenora's face and was surprised at how swollen her face appeared in the dimmed lighting. "Oh well, my pretty. You aren't going anywhere of any importance real soon, anyway."

She picked up her cell phone and called her daughter and cohort in the ultra-subtle kidnapping of Lenora Moore.

"Hello! Tammy? It's mom..."

"How did it go, mom?"

"She's a real angel. I slipped her an ounce of loboci-duce with the sweet Jamaicans."

"Oh mother! You didn't! Did it work?"

"Yes, it works. I'm here to tell you, sweetie. It works beyond any imagination."

"I'll be right there, mom. Should I bring Robert?"

"No! No Robert! I don't want him anywhere around here. Have him wait for us on the boat."

"Ok... I'll be there in ten minutes." And the connection was severed.

Nancy removed Lenora's pearls. Robert had said that they had cost him a bundle. They would look very nice around her daughter's long neck; she could envision them on her as clear as if she were looking at a freshly printed color photograph.

Lenora moaned something about being thirsty and Nancy said she'd get her a fresh drink shortly, as soon as her daughter Tammy arrived; a nice Palm Frond Rum special. And then to her self, she thought ...it'll be the last drink you'll ever taste, my little pretty.

Tammy let herself in. She made her way back to the napping room and entered, her mother had dressed, all in black, and was sitting on the bed stroking Lenora's silky ass. Lenora was coherent and enjoying the tender rub, "I'm so thirsty. Oh, that feels so nice. Oh, why is my tongue so swollen?" Her delirium was steadfast and her ability to move was near comatose.

Tammy approached the bed and touched Lenora, "Jesus! She's ice cold, mom. And just look at her face..."

Nancy fluffed at her hair, "If you want to play with her, go ahead. But we need to get this over with pretty quick. Is it dark out yet?"

"Yes. Traffic is sparse. There are a few people out walking. But it'll be dead soon."

"Nice choice of words, Tammy."

"Oh. Well... You know what I mean."

Tammy rolled Lenora over and studied her body, "Damn! She's a ten from the top on down, mom." I see what Robert saw in her. She's beautiful. He said she was a nice person, too."

"She's cute. You're beautiful, Tammy. Believe in yourself, sweetie."

"So she just showed up at the lounge? You never called her? I guess Robert left enough clues to make her suspect our affair without you calling her to tip her off."

"When I called their house there was no answer. That's when I hurried over to the Hancock. I watched her approach your table and throw down the dildo. That's when I went to the little girl's room. I knew she'd go there. There wasn't anywhere left for her to turn."

"You're good, mom. So, what do we do now?"

"Well... She's out of it for another good two hours. We just walk her out as if she's drunk. Take her down to the boat. Go out about a mile and... Dump her. Just remember, sweetie, if we get caught, it's Robert who's going to take the heat, not me or you. I don't care how much you love him. Ok?"

"Ok. Mom, I really appreciate this."

"I know you do. Ok. Let's get her dressed and out of here."

A MIDNIGHT SAIL

Robert had Nancy's 26-foot sloop, Pirouette, ready to sail. In a matter of seconds he could throw off the mooring lines and hoist the mainsail. The light northwest prevailing winds would have them past the breakwater in less then ten minutes, without ever having to tack or jibe. No engine, no sound; no attention would be drawn to their late night departure.

It was almost midnight when Nancy's burgundy Mercedes pulled up to the sea wall and parked a mere fifteen yards from the softly lapping waves that bust up against the length of the concrete pier and the fiberglass hull of the only boat moored there, the Pirouette. No one was about and the walking lanes were completely clear. A small sliver moon was barely noticeable in the dark but star studded, cloudless sky.

Robert had a light on in the teak lined cabin but was up on deck smoking a cigarette when the three women approached. He helped them get his wife, Lenora, below and Nancy went off to park the car.

Robert was shaken at the sight of his wife. He had loved her passionately and deeply, that is until he met the sex kitten, Tammy. And when he met Tammy's mother, Nancy, it was a match made in banking heaven.

With Robert's banking knowledge and Nancy's legal manipulations of law over her client's laundered money, they had embezzled nearly thirty million dollars in three hectic months of shuffling corporate and family funds around the world and into their own personal offshore account. It was brilliant! It was too easy! And, when Robert fell in love with Nancy's daughter, Tammy; Lenora became a damn loose end to their clandestine scheme and his need and want of Tammy.

Nancy returned from parking the car and Robert helped her aboard. The lines were cast and the sails were hoisted. Robert set the jib and Nancy took the wheel. Robert almost forgot to turn on the mast and transom lights, but got them on within a minute after his jib lines snapped tight into the starboard cam cleat. In a downwind run the sloop was set solid for a beeline out into the open waters of Lake Michigan.

Robert took the wheel and Nancy went below to check on Tammy and Lenora.

"Why don't you go up with Bobby? He's really tense. I'll hold Lenora's hand until we're past the breakwater."

Tammy was in a somber state and didn't answer. She just stood and went up the hatch. The black moment of truth was nearing and Tammy was scared which was unlike her usual confident self. She had never actually killed anyone before. She was trembling when she reached her Robert, "I don't know if I can do this, Bobby. Do we have to dispose of her?"

"Yes, Tam. She's going overboard. It's too late now. We have millions of dollars. She'd screw everything up. She's got to go... Don't worry, Tam. Everything's going to work out just fine, you'll see."

Robert passed the break wall and the water became a bit choppier. He had Tammy man the jib and brought the sailboat into a reach heading north. He started to freak out as the waves were really bouncing them about. He decided to use the engine and drop the sails. The city lights, the magnificent skyline of Chicago was never as beautiful as this to him in his whole entire life. Excitement and terror gripped his soul simultaneously, the moment of truth; the time for murder was suddenly a blatant reality.

Nancy heard the engine start and knew the sails would be lowered... "Are you ready for that drink, Lenora? How about some nice cold water? Doesn't that sound nice?"

Lenora was still stupefied but understood and nodded out an agreement to the cold-water offer. Then, an awareness surged through her and she felt fear, something was dead wrong. She wanted to run away. She didn't want to be wherever she was and her mouth was so dry... It hurt to even open it. And her tongue was so swollen, too.

"What 'ith going on?" she tried asking through pained and fattened lips. She needed something to drink. "I'm thir-tee," came out in a mumble of hurt sound.

And then she tried standing, but quickly fell back to the padded seat and stared blankly at Nancy, "I ... Hate you."

Nancy stood and bent over Lenora, and began to get her to stand with a rough tug up on her arms, "Come on, sweetie. Let's go get that drink of water. It's just up these stairs a few feet and you can have all the nice cold water in the whole wide world. How does that sound?"

Lenora could barely stand; with the boat rocking and her drug-induced instability she somehow made it to the aft stairwell, guided roughly – albeit brutally by Nancy, "Up you go! Come on sweetie, one step at a time."

"I... I feel like I'm going to--" and before she could speak the word, Lenora vomited, violently.

Nancy was immediately splattered heavily from her arms to her feet, "Oh! You bitch!" and she began pushing Lenora upward like one would do to rid themselves of an overstuffed garbage bag.

Robert came to the hatch to assist, "Hi Len. Let me help you." And he reached her arms and tugged her up and onto the aft deck getting her regurgitated innards all over his hands, shoes, and pants. He let go of her and she crumpled hard to the teak flooring. Nancy's head came out of the cuddy and Robert could see the goop dripping on her face and neck even in the darkness.

"Get her ass over, Robert!" Nancy screamed, "Do it! Now!"

Robert grabbed Lenora under the arms and tried not to look at her, but he did. His heart was pounding and he was trying not to breathe because of the fruity stench. His hands slipped briefly and he looked her full in her pleading eyes as he readjusted his grip, "Oh Len... I'm so sorry." And with those words he heaved her over the transom.

Lenora felt the cold water surround her and made a feeble attempt to swim, but she had no energy and went under still staring at her Robert who was leaning on the rail watching her go down. Nancy and Tammy joined him in a fuzzy image and Lenora closed her eyes not wanting the evil trio to be her last view of life. She couldn't hold her breath any longer and released the air out from her aching lungs.

She felt the water entering her nose and mouth, and her life ending.

Nancy climbed down the aluminum swimming ladder and began washing herself off. Tammy had shut off the engine when Robert shouted at her to do so.

Robert just stood there looking into the black water, glad that he'd never have to hear his wife's whining voice ever again.

EPILOGUE

A few days passed before anyone was missed to the point of someone calling the police. But they were eventually called. The four missing person reports are now filed in a cold case file somewhere in Chicago.

Lenora's body never surfaced. Nancy's sailboat was abandoned along with her offices and lakeshore condo. The Moore house went back to the bank as an abandoned property. Blake, the basketball-playing neighbor missed Lenora more than Robert did.

Robert and Tammy were set to married in a small beachside ceremony in Argentina one year later. There were no invitations sent out. No one in the world knew who, or where, they were. Except for Nancy, who got drunk one night and made a phone call to one of her ex's in Nevada. She just had to brag how she had finally hit the jackpot.

Nancy would serve happily as Tammy's Matron of Honor. Yes, she would stand proudly next to her cohorts in crime during their illicit exchange of vows. Her smile would be mistaken for a sardonic grin as she would admire the pearls that her daughter would wear, after all, they were so suited for her daughter's long neck, unlike Robert's bitch, Lenora; who only liked to sit around and read romance novels.

On the eve of this fateful wedding, two burly Italian men wearing thousand dollar suits checked into a nearby beach front hotel overlooking the gazebo where Robert and Tammy were to be wed. Their "invitation" to the Robert Morris and Tammy Farmington nuptials came via an unknown source in Las Vegas. It simply said, "Kill 'em all."

The End!

Story 3: Seducing the Boss

Introduction

My name is Taylor, Taylor O. Blake; the "O" according to my ex-boyfriend stands for oversexed. Now, with that little tidbit aside, I'm compelled to tell you my personal inside story. A true tale of how a little bit of sexual promiscuity, straight or gay, can change one's life -- forever. This all happened – only one week ago. And now, without guilt, without shame, and without consequence from God or any living human being -- my story now unfolds...

Chapter One

It was a warm June evening. A Friday night, and I found myself home...alone, again. My boyfriend, Richard, was away on business, a trip to France. He travels there, to Champagne, often, on behalf of his company, "Wines of Europe," as a buyer in the wine import industry. And me, I work 9-5 as a web-advertising consultant. Basically, I purchase ad spots for start-up businesses.

My boss, Sally Anderson, treats me like a genuine goddess, and I – well, I've secretly fallen in love with her. For years, I've looked at her with a seductive eye and yet, somehow, I've controlled my deeply hidden sexual wants and desires for her. Mostly by satisfying my latent and ever festering carnal needs for her -- through my lover, Richard. How many nights I had lain at his side and pretended that he, muscle building Richard, was my Sally with her soft and plushy breast snuggled up warm and tight against me.

I found many ways to stop myself from seducing her, ways to control my urges to be intimate with her. Oh, I've felt these feelings before, with others, but this was a whole new chemistry that enveloped me toward Sally and it was simply maddening. My boss, my beloved, was just too damned straight!

Turning off the TV, I went to my bedroom and stripped naked. I stood looking at myself in an old antique full-length mirror. I liked what I saw. My breasts were firm and, I must say, well naturally proportioned. As I ran my hands over them – my nipples responded and formed a pair of dark magenta thimbles that poked up from the aureole centers; a small mystery this wee formation, one that still amuses me when they are touched or kissed or suckled upon.

Turning my butt to the glass, I looked over my shoulder and studied my ass. This pleasant view convinced me that my exercise routines were worth all the time and effort that I spent to keep myself nicely contoured. I could see that my flesh was firm and totally cellulite free. Yes, firm but my skin felt soft and oh so smooth to my own touch. I let my hands press gently around the silky cheeks and it felt nice, very nice. I felt a small pang of arousal and that too was nice.

I turned back and eyed myself further fixating on my tummy; I'm an inny, and a cute inny as far as navels go... My hands toured my hips and then I focused on my pubic patch of auburn strands and felt the hairs playfully with my fingertips. I begin fondling my pussy mound as I watched, amused, and thoughtless of what I was doing and of my immediate surroundings. With both hands I exposed the pink flesh of my clitoral appendage, and then a euphoric wave of pleasure engulfed my senses as I made little light circles around my now fully extended clitoris.

Moisture developed as my fingers toyed in with gentle, and deliberate, sensitive, plunges between the folds of my titillated flesh. A heavy breath, my own, and a deep inhale had signaled my increasing passion to reach self-gratification. And my thoughts took off on an instant excursion to a mental picture of my latest friend and lover, Richard. Rich, with his chiseled facial features now hovered flush over my upward gyrating, grinding pussy, his mouth suckled gently all around and everywhere about my clitoris and then he lapped his tongue in tempo to my quickening fevered pitch and to his own orgasmic-prompted oral madness.

And then he'd stop ever so briefly. He'd softly whisper to me how, superb, my juices tasted. Then, with those soft, but exacting, echoes of past lovemaking racing through my head, I swiped my own two middle fingers deep and firm up into my moistened vagina and retracted them, wet, covered deliciously with my own sticky love serum. Then placed them, one by one, hungrily into my trembling mouth where I licked each of them to a tasty and hygienic cleanliness, and then reached down for yet more.

Euphoric, I moved to the bed and sprawled out with my legs spread open and my knees elevated and I thought more on how Richard had these special ways -- with his mouth -- that no man (or woman) before or after him could ever come close to matching. His skill, his timing, and the amount of pressure that he applied were always measured and always just beyond that cutting edge of giving pleasure as an act of perfection. His sexual game was to please and, I'm here to attest, he always won! I always let him...

I softly gripped my pussy and made my Mound de Venus flesh move in a circular direction. With my other hand stroking lightly across my breasts and down the length of my tanned torso and then back up, over and over again and again in rapid movements that fired my skin to new highs of self-indulgent pleasure. And then – with an uncontrolled and sudden spasm, my body arched upward and my thighs tightened about my hand and an unearthly euphoria permeated through every cell of my incarnate being. An uncontrollable scream rose unbridled from the depths of my satisfaction center, up and out it came -- a cry of pure fulfilled lust and uninhibited jubilation.

And then this strange feeling, a passion, over-whelmed me, and a three-dimensional vision of my co-worker, Sally (Sunshine) Peterson enveloped my every throbbing sense. She was naked before me and she – seemed -- so very, very real. I reached the light on the nightstand and turned it on. The vision ended. My God! My boss appearing to me nude and in an erotic pose of touch me, feel me, see me...and with that flash of light, the vision was dispelled. All of that beautiful vividness out of my, what should have been -- sexually satiated mind.

I laughed to myself and then questioned my own sexual orientation. Why was I seeing, imagining, my best friend Sally? Naked! I just didn't have an answer. But as I thought a little deeper on it, I came up with a few plausible and completely pleasurable ideas.

Sal is a naturally sexy woman. She dresses like a 200-dollar hooker and always smells like a 500-dollar whore. She's married to a genuine hunk, James, a guy so suave he sends her a flower every day of the goddamned week. And when he visits our office, it's always, "My little bird." Or "Baby Sweets." Or he'll walk in and kiss her full on the mouth – too long, and he rubs her ass right in front of my face, that bastard.

One day, she, Sally, actually asked if I'd go some-where for twenty-minutes so she could give sweetie a quick blowjob. And me, I left... Now, who's the fool on that one? So. I deliberately came back in ten minutes, and I caught her, on her knees, and him all smiles zipping up his pants like nothing had ever happened. So, James says to me, quietly so Sal can't hear, "What? You never sucked a dick during business hours?" Then he smiles a sick smile and walks out; leaving me red-faced in front of Sal.

Sal heard, even though she wasn't supposed to. She says to me, "I'm glad you came back early, Taylor. Another minute and he'd have shot his wad and... I would have had to swallow. We're out of Kleenex," she said, smiling through her slightly swollen lips. But even that, she did with élan. Brushed it off as an office chore and goes right back to being pretty and proudly taking care of business.

Oh! ...I had read a copy of Playboy, one that Richard had left lying around, this was earlier that evening, too. That, coupled with the fact that Richard was on an extended stay over in France for the last three weeks and not due back for another two... Well, maybe – just maybe, I do hold some latent lesbian desires, especially for Sal.

Okay! I do hold these strange feelings. And at that very moment, I turned off the bed-lamp and fell back down on my green silk designer sheets. Naked, with my hand resting loosely atop my still vibrant pussy, I regained my vision of Sally kneeling above my face. I closed my eyes with the picture of her clit exposed above me and I swear it literally made my mouth water. The last waking thought that I held that night was, "I have to seduce Sally... I will seduce Sally – Cum on, Monday morning."

Chapter Two

When I woke on Saturday, I had slept in until 9 a.m., I felt fresh and then recalled dreaming of Richard. His penis was exposed to me sticking out of the zipper hole of his pants. It was erect and oh so hard. The purple tip had a single drop of oozed semen protruding from his little penis hole. I tried to move forward to lick it away, but every time I did, it would retract back, all the way back, right into his pants. When I'd withdraw from my attempt, the penis would come out again. This went on as a recurring sequence until I finally lunged forward and caught his shiny bulb in my drooling lips. I sucked around the head and tasted the salty excretion on my taste buds. Oh my God, it was so titillating! I engulfed him as deep as I could and took over half of his cock full into my mouth.

He began to throb -- his penis began to throb, full out as I clamped down on his ready to ejaculate peter head and rolled my tongue over his, now gushing, sperm. And he did, he exploded full into my ready and willing mouth. And then, the dream changed!

Richard's penis became Sally's clitoris, and her beautiful juices poured out into my mouth and oozed down my chin, to my neck, and down onto the silk bedding. There was so much! And it tasted so wonderfully delicious. I pulled her tight against my face and went into orgasm on my own -- without even being touched. And then, I woke...

I had actually drooled in my sleep. Something I never do. I looked at my pillows and at the damp sheets and began laughing. Jesus Christ! I even looked to see if Sally was indeed in my bed – hiding under my covers. The dream was that vivid! I lay there in a slight post-orgasmic pant. I relived the dream several more times; until it vanished from my cognizant, short memory. Parts of the dream still lingered: Richard's beautiful prick and the sheen of its tight bulbous tip; that tasty lone drop of his semen; and the cum explosion into my wanton mouth... But the best part, Sally's clit between my lips – well, I have that part locked in my long-term memory now. I have recalled that fantastic scene a hundred times since then, and I'm sure I'll go there often in the future, Yes, as a recollection worth a million dollars... Ah, such a tasty, tasty dream.

The sheets had to be changed and the pillowcases, too. But it was all worth it. I headed for the shower still vibrant and, yes! Damp between my legs, too.

I took a long soaking shower. I soaped my breasts in a fondling zest. I was feeling so alive just thinking of Sally. But, when I lathered my pussy with my scented soap bar, my thoughts turned to Richard and his nine-inch penis.

Dragging the cake of soap slowly across my pelvis, I wished it were Richard's stiffness and not a bar of scented soap. I remember talking to the soap, "How'd that feel, Mister Bubbles?" and I laughed. And actually had a pang, an erotic pulse, which shot up my newly lubricated vagina. I moved Mister Bubbles to my ass and smeared the softening bar up my crack, twisting the soap a bit, getting the bar's edge slightly up my hole and then – massaged there with my fingertips.

This felt pleasant and with the soap as a lubricant I entered myself for a brief moment of anal arousal. It was nice. It made me recall the first time that Richard fucked me in the ass. I was afraid, then. Yet – I found myself enjoying his sexual perversion. But, no pun intended, I no longer view this ass-act as being so perverse, it's just a little bit -- unconventional?

I spread my legs in a slight squat and turned the showerhead to pulse and let the water jets rinse about my pelvis. It felt so nice, so warm... I let the water beat against my thighs and made circular moves with the head and the contoured molding of the flexible spray nozzle. My thoughts raced to Sally's beautiful mouth and I pretended that the pressure I felt was from her lips caressing my labia and teasing my exposed, and now, highly sensitive clitoris, and I did this -- right into orgasm. Damn! It felt so powerful, so sexually rewarding, and I stayed there until the water no longer ran warm and I only turned off the faucet when I felt a slight shiver from the cold – cold water.

Dab drying with an ultra-soft cotton towel I seriously wondered if Sally would, indeed, succumb to my sexual advances. I wanted her. I wanted to touch her. I wanted to lock lips, and dart my tongue into her mouth. I wanted her to be responsive to my fondling of her breasts and my gripping her gorgeous ass. I wanted to hear her moan as I pulled on her clitoris with my lips and feel her tremor with delight as I ran the tip of my tongue back and forth across her ass hole while grasping her firm ass with one hand and delving into her pussy with the other – I wanted her to scream! To scream out in an esoteric freedom of pleasurable delight, to scream out from every gentle touch of my feminine hands and every one of my pampering finger manipulations. And I had to squeeze my thighs together on these pleasurable thoughts that had encompassed me. As I dried, out loud, and for my own benefit, I sang out, "I am going to fuck you, Sally! And I'm going to enjoy every fucking moment of it."

Chapter Three

My masturbating had left me tender around the outer fringes of my pussy. My clitoris was overworked to the point that my touching it was no longer a pleasure. I laughed at my own foolishness as I was still in a desirous mood, a mood to experience more physical arousal – I was in that numb state of mentally wanting, needing, to have further sexual feelings expressed -- the pleasure of satisfaction, and having it right then -- all by myself.

I applied a soothing gel, a new skin softener, one that came in a penis-sized applicator. The blue translucent cream turned invisible upon contact with my flesh. The effect of the wintergreen scent and the tingling, soothing, properties of the product immediately eased the soreness that I was, up to then, unfortunately experiencing.

Climbing into bed with the gel tube in hand, just in case, I fluffed my pillows and snuggled in for a restful sleep. And I did sleep -- deep and sound. And I dreamt...

Richard was in my office. He was seducing Sally on top of Sal's desk while I worked on a monthly statistical report, junk for posterity. I tried to ignore their brash display but they kept looking at me to ensure that I was taking in every one of their grunts and groans. And then Sally's husband walks in.

He comes walking across the floor and right up to my desk and whispers to me, while pointing a thumb toward Richard and Sally, "What's that all about, Taylor?" and he has this big smile glued across his face and he was more concerned with observing my cleavage than challenging his wife as to why she was madly fucking my boyfriend's brains out right there in the office.

And then I'm walking hand in hand with James toward Sally's desk. Richard's bare ass is rising and falling as he pumps hard and sweaty into Sally who is observing our approach with a snickering grin that is at the same time issuing audible grunts in tune to Richard's plunges.

James reaches out his hand and places it on Richard's tightened butt and pats it, saying, "Slow down there my boy, slow down," as we stood alongside the desk still holding hands and just watched. Then Sally claws Richard's back in a frenzied display of orgasmatic pleasure that shoots through her torso. Her face contorts in a pleasure-scream and is then joined instantly with the voice of Richard extolling his own orgasmatic expletives to his own God as some form of thank you to his own asexual universe and his own moment of pure and unadulterated male ecstasy.

The dream ends with me rubbing Sally's pussy, smearing all the shared jissum that they exuded so methodically and jointly, into, over, and all around her bushy and now gooey blonde pussy hair. And then I woke. And... Saturday was upon the dawn and I didn't find my tube of ointment until I entered the confines of my shower and there it was, by golly. This gave me a hearty laugh as I extracted the comforting penis form from between my still tender labia lips. And it made me laugh...

.

Chapter Four

Richard called me from Europe. I had just finished blow-drying my hair after that leisurely morning shower. There I stood, naked, chit chatting with the blower in one hand and my cell in the other. He said he was just going to bed. It was late there, in Champagne, and he complained that he had tasted way too many samples of the local wines. And then, I heard a faint giggle in the background.

"Richard, is there someone with you?"

"Don't be silly, sweetheart. No. There isn't anyone here but me."

"There damn well better not be, Richard." and before I could finish, the line went dead. "Richard! Richard? Are you there, baby?"

Needless to say, that little conversation started my day off on a very sour note. That bastard was with another woman! It really pissed me off, too. He was only gone for two, three weeks and he couldn't keep his dick holstered for a mere fourteen more days. Damn him! Frustrated, I finished drying my hair with a full-blown fury. Something was going on in France. Richard was fucking around. I distinctly heard the background giggles. And, I just wasn't buying the snap disconnection. Why do men have to be like this? He has such a beautiful, intelligent, and outgoing woman – me. Yet he's going to go over there and fuck around. I was working up a jealous streak and it was becoming quite maddening.

* * *

An aside... During Richard's stateside call to Taylor, a fourteen-year-old French hussy, one that claimed to be eighteen, was sucking off Richard's nine-inch penis. As she poked a finger full up Richard's ass she simultaneously grasped his balls with her other hand. The consequence was a premature orgasm smack into her un-expecting youthful mouth. This happened at the exact moment that Richard had to sever his oversea connection. Yes. Had to!

Mimi laughed aloud as his cum ran down her chin and began a thick milky coating on her tiny, but well formed, teenage breasts. Mimi had never experienced such a copious flow from any of her Parisian boyfriends. With excitement, she then proceeded to suck up every last explosive drop of Dick's still warm and saline laced cum. This was all happening about the time his cell phone lid was excitedly snapped down to sever their connection. Richard yelled out in climax, American style, "Oh, God damn, Mimi!" so loud, that management was called to his room to investigate a domestic violence call; one that was made to the hotel's desk clerk shortly after Richard climaxed.

Mimi was excited. Ha! She was exuberant, with her juvenile adventure. She immediately insisted that she give Dick a second, consecutive, orgasm via her talented tongue and her manipulative handwork. To which -- Richard had readily and greedily agreed.

Several minutes later, when management entered without knocking, Richard went into climax, again, for the second time. Mimi in a dreamy trance of pure pleasure, heard the (illegal?) entry and looked to the door... With cum oozing from her slightly swollen lips, she, gagging, exclaimed, "Papa!"

The American Embassy is trying to get Richard back to the states as this is being written. Poor Richard...

* * *

Angry and frustrated by Richard's call, I dressed comfy in a light skirt and a deep v-neck top. Deliberately, I abandoned my panties and it made me feel sexy beyond all get-outs. Some lucky guy was going to get an eyeful somewhere along the line, and I promised myself that it wouldn't be a simple accident. Then, in the same breath, I added, "Fuck you Richard." And then thought about Sally, my lovely, beautiful Sally.

On the way downtown, I was cognizant of the leather seat grasping my ass. I wished it was Sally and in the windshield, I envisioned her undressed and allowing me to suck her breasts and let me kiss up and down her flat tummy and letting me dart my tongue into her delta of honey sweetened oozing pussy flesh. And a horn blared loudly as a huge delivery truck came up along side of my passenger door. The driver was grinning like a hog in an apple patch as he loomed at my crotch with bugged-out eyes. My hand was up my skirt and it made me happy that the fat-fuck driver had noticed. I smiled and winked over in the trucks direction. Then, I slowed and deliberately allowed him to pass.

Regaining the image of Sally in my minds eye, I knelt before her – gripping her ass, I pulled her pussy into my wanton lips, and I swear, my mouth watered, and I literally darted out my tongue to enter her juicy portal of pleasure. But the light turned yellow ahead of me and the thoughts – so beautiful as they were – vanished into the reality of heavy traffic and the need to drive safe.

Two blocks later, I was at Flassiddio's Dress Shoppe, a high-end shop where all the swanky hookers buy their toxic street wear, the clothes that make a man go erect before he even notices that you have a really fine ass and serious cleavage, a cleavage that makes a man want to go deeper than the bottom of the Grand Canyon itself.

It was ten-o-clock sharp, they had just opened, and a young girl asked me if I needed assistance. She was so damned cute, Jesus! I thought, "Yes! Honey baby, you could assist me, right into an orgasm, by my just looking at you."

Recklessly, looking at her seductive curves that were all amply exposed by a watermelon colored outfit, I asked if she'd show me something like the whore dress she was personally wearing. And then – to my own surprise, I reached out and touched the cloth that enwrapped her plush, and openly exhibited erect nipples, breasts, and inquired, "Silk?"

Smiling playfully, ignoring my touch to her top, she eyed me from head to toe. "Yes, it's silk. I just love it." and then she quickly suggested, "It comes in several colors, and I'm sure we have a size six. You are a size six, aren't you?"

"Yes. A sex. I mean, six." And then I found myself saying, "You are a very beautiful young woman." I reached the hem of her short skirt and grasping it, I felt the material, also a silk, but not a real glossy one. I slightly lifted the hem and as I did so I felt this wonderful rush of blood flush up to my face – I had observed that Little Miss Big Tits wasn't wearing any panties either, and I swear, she had a hopeful shadow of lust flash across her face when I looked up at her. She allowed herself to turn dreamy eyed, and then her powder blue eyes gave it all up, as she squinted with an accepted knowledge of her own need. And we both smiled. And in that quick but deep moment of stark wonderment -- we both knew.

She helped me strip naked in the four-mirror fitting-room. She then ordered me (very dyke like) to sit on the padded bench. To which, I gladly and oh so willingly, did. I had already succumbed to her dominance, I was now her bitch, and I'd do anything and everything she wished. It wasn't discussed, it wasn't negotiated, it was intuitive and I wanted it, badly, and went with the mystery.

Her silk hit the floor, floated to the floor, like the parachute material that it was and exposed the most beautiful pussy that I had ever seen, anywhere, and I had spent some nice time viewing pussy on the Internet.

She moved into my face and I took her hungrily between my lips. She grabbed my hair and guided my head forcefully, but gently flush, against her gyrating hips. She then lifted a leg to the bench to give her pussy more space and my tongue a clearer entry. And she poured, sakes alive she spewed, love juices almost faster than I could swallow, it was so delicious! She was unbelievably – aah, was just dripping fantastic. I dug my nails into her butt and pulled her tight and I felt her shake in the bold tremors of an unstoppable orgasm. It made me feel so alive to be giving her such a powerful and unabashed release.

She put her leg down and we kissed magnificent kisses as she fondled my breast and hardened up my nipples. Then, she ordered me to bend over the bench and offer up my ass -- to her mouth. And – Oh my God! She had her head flush full against my ass and her tongue was entering my asses hole with the fastest in and out movement that I never thought was humanly possible.

Then, while tonguing me, she reaches around and grabs my entire pelvic area and starts this tender grind with both hands. I knew I was soaking her hands in natural lubricants and it felt so fucking wonderful – I wanted to just scream. She then ran one hand up and down my tummy and I just exploded in horrific ecstasy. I mean – I saw stars! I saw rainbows. I shot right up through the entire Milky Way's milk and landed smack dab back down on Venus. And we kissed again, deep and hungry, and she smiled a knowing smile that she had reciprocated beyond all belief the pleasures that I had just extended onto her. And we dressed, and I purchased a cream-colored-silk-whore's-outfit for four hundred dollars.

As I staggered out to my Lexus I felt a secondary shudder of continuing orgasmic, after shocks! I placed the pink shopping bag on the passenger's seat and then stared at the clerk's home phone number, the only thing that she quickly scrawled on back of the store's business card. I never asked her for her name. It simply hadn't come up. But, I had her number... And as I pulled out of the parking lot, I noticed her waving at me from behind the store's mauve tinted window. As I pulled into my driveway, still vibrant from my nips to my clit, I recall, saying this out loud, "Fuck you Richard! You've been replaced, Mister Dick."

Wearing my new outfit, I inspected my new image in the full-length mirror. I was hot. The skimpy dress made me look like I was ready for anything; as long as it was sexual.

And then I pretended that I was Sally looking at me, Taylor, and I thought, how could Sally not want to have sex with me? It was a sure thing; we were as good as in bed, almost. "Hurry Monday!" was now my battle cry. I would seduce her and life would be beautiful – forever.

Chapter Five

I spent all day Sunday healing all the tender spots of my sexual being. I worked in the garden and pulled every weed that showed its ugly self. I pondered Richard with disdain; every thought I ever had of marrying him was being thrown out now; along with my pile of discarded weeds.

About eight that night I took a long, soothing, scented bath. I would smell like a jasmine forest come morning, and I'd be as clean as a kitchen plate fresh out of the dishwasher, just for Sally's pleasure. As I soaked, I practiced mentally how I'd approach her. It would work. It had to work! My love was too strong for it not to work. And then I crawled into bed. I began to contemplate what had happened at Flassiddio's.

The Shoppe, the fitting room, and 555-6969 aroused me. Just thinking about it made me warm, made me glow with passion. Suddenly, I was masturbating with my night-stand adjunct, my vibrator (I have named it, Mickey). And I fell asleep with the damn thing buzzing away against my clitoris.

Monday morning arrived; I dressed to the nines, dabbed on my best (90 dollar an ounce) scent, fluffed up my hair, and headed for my destiny – Sally. The new outfit felt great and it made me feel like a million bucks. I wore my beige sandals with the narrow heel strap and weaved open toes; because, they kick off very nicely. I was all set. I matched; and I knew that I was an icon of pure sexuality.

Sally's car, a gun barrel-blue Mercedes convertible, was already in the lot when I arrived. The top was down and I thought this a good thing as a sign of her free-spirited nature. I parked my silver Lexus next to hers as a personal display of coziness. Then -- with all the confidence of a Chief Justice, I entered the office.

Sally was seated at her desk drinking a carried in Starbucks coffee, the Monday Morning Moocow, as we had come to call it. Mine was ready on my desk. Sally always bought on Mondays; it was ritualistic.

My dress was noticed immediately, "Wow! Look at you, Taylor. Have a date after work? I thought Richard was out of town?"

I braved myself and boldly stated, "I dressed up for you, Sal." I walked to her desk and modeled my wares, "Do you like?"

Sal removed her reading glasses and took a hard look at what I was offering. She had a coy smile form on her lips and just froze there and ogled me. And I knew I felt her seeing me as an available sexual entity. It sent me into a breathing pant, a pant of desire. I felt like a wild animal, a panther in heat waiting to mate, instantly, right there, right on the jungle's floor.

I blurted out, "I love you Sally."

Sally's mouth opened very slightly. She was about to say something, something wonderful! But nothing came out of her mouth, no words. Nada! Nothing... She just stared at me with her beautiful mouth hanging wide open and looking so damn gorgeous.

Tears began to well up in my eyes; I stammered out the words, "I want...to ...make love with you, Sal."

* * *

Everything after that was pandemonium. Expletives flew out of Sal's mouth like machinegun bullets. Words about the wrath of hell echoed around the office walls and probably still are, as I sit here and write this down, today. I was then fired, right on the spot. Those horrible words

"Get out! And don't you ever come back." are now etched into my brain for the rest of eternity.

I passed James on his way in as I made my last trip out from loading my personal things into my car. Sally had called him to come to her side. I remember his last word, the one he foolishly said to me, "ARF!" That was the ugly bastard's only remark. I think he was just imitating himself, as a mad dog, in animalistic heat.

On Tuesday, I called the 555-6969 number and asked if there were any job openings. There were. On Wednesday, I interviewed extensively -- in the fitting room. On Thursday, I was officially hired after answering a few follow up questions, which were presented, in the fitting room. On Friday, I worked my first day with Barbara, my brand new boss, and (of course) my newest lover.

The End!

STORY 4: VASSAR GIRL

CHAPTER 1

Mark, my fiancé, was on his knees licking my pussy as I hurriedly brushed out my bed-tangled hair.

"I'm going to be late but I could really use an orgasm so don't stop. Harder! Lower! Higher! Deeper! In! Out!" I threw my head back and suddenly didn't give a shit about my hair as I neared orgasm. Then the phone rang. "Shit!"

Mark lifted his head, "Just leave it babe!"

I knew I had to answer the phone. This close to walking the stage, it could've been anyone calling with something important.

"Hello?" My voice was quivering though I tried to sound nonchalant.

"Honey?" he questioned — as if he'd never heard my voice before, "Is that you, baby doll?"

"Yes daddy, it's me." I replied with a distinct edge in my voice. I was running late and really didn't have time to be chitchatting with my shipping magnate father, not to mention Mark was still down under. "Sweetie...   an emergency just came up... I'll make it up to you... Here's your mother." Mom, the latest patron saint of Wall Street, rattled on for five minutes as to why daddy had to not only get off the phone but leave Vassar for an emergency business meeting in the city. It wasn't anything I hadn't heard before. She always made excuses for him. The wording was different but the message was the same, "...business before pleasure." My thoughts of experiencing an orgasm vanished faster than my father's current presence in Vassar's Pratt House. I asked Mark to stop licking me. My elated mood was broken; and besides, I had to be on stage in less than twenty minutes – my sheepskin needed me! I learned that one in one of my earlier Existential Philosophy classes. After all, one does have to study something when one attends Vassar. I sent puffy-lipped Mark out the door with an erection bulging in his K-Mart khaki's. If I only had had ten more minutes... I would have put a very large smile on his face, and mine, for the rest of the day. But, graduation is graduation. I pulled on my graduation gown over my naked body. Damn that felt good. I wondered how many other audacious graduates would be nude under their robes.

With a quick glance at myself in the bedroom door's mirror, and a slip on of my high heel shoes, I entered the dorm hallway. It was a mad house; I wasn't the only one racing to the Outdoor Amphitheater. Angela and the Physics freak Kelly joined me in a hustle to exit the front door. We were friends for life, and all three of us were on the verge of being unforgivably late.

Late May in the Hudson Valley of New York happens to be the most perfect place on God's green earth. The scent of apple blossoms wafted all about the sprawling campus and would continue well into June. How did we ever study surrounded by all this magnificent beauty was the only thought in my mind as we raced to the festivities.

Charles Von Klopp, a junior majoring in Mathematics, stepped out from a group of students and blocked my way with his beautiful German smile, "Congratulations frauline," his accent shot a shiver up my spine as I recalled him seducing me so successfully, two years earlier.

I remember the seduction well, how could I ever forget it? We had been, each separately, strolling around the grounds looking for a place to read. I had a Jane Austin novel and he was carrying a Gunter Grass, an English version. We met, talked a few minutes, and then sat down together on the fresh mown lawn. He read a few passages from the "Tin Drum" aloud and I threw out some "Pride and Prejudice" lines out to his fully attuned ear. It was fun. We laughed. The sun begun to set, and we just sat there and listened to crickets chirp in the twilight; and, neither of us spoke a word. Lights burned bright in the surrounding dorms and I wished upon the first star that began to flicker dimly above Charles' blond hair. And my wish came true as he moved his head onto my neck and kissed me with a small lip-nip below my ear.

More stars filled the heavens as the moonless evening closed in and wrapped us in a blanket of wantonness. His hands were warm and he moved them so softly about my flesh... I found his belt buckle and soon heard his zipper descend with a tug from my eager fingers. I felt his penis grow in the palm of my hand as I set it free from the tightness of his briefs. All the while he was unleashing my bra and letting his tongue invade my willing mouth. And then we were bare, clothed in nothing but a starry night and a warm patch of grass below our glowing bodies. An observant owl hooted in the distance as Charles entered me, slow and deliberate, and oh, he was so hard and his thrusts were so gentle... Charles was speaking softly in German. It was guttural, but universally understood – he was in orgasm. His final lunge made me explode in a body tightening frenzy of unheralded passion.

My nails raked along his back as he arched out of my juices and then he slowly came back into me and I locked his still throbbing penis tight in my vulva. And then he rolled away onto his side, panting, and then he laughed. It was a soothing laugh, a loving show of enjoyment over what had just happened. And we both became breathlessly silent; we were at a luxurious peace with our individual selves.

On that night, I knew – as I looked skyward and took in the majesty of nature's sparkling heaven – what it meant to be sexually satiated. It was a splendid moment of my informal education. I prayed that night, too. I remember quite distinctly thanking God for such a wonderful experience, and then asking Him (God) to not let me become pregnant.

We dressed then, without speaking. Not one single word was spoken. I picked up my Jane Austin book and Charles picked up his Gunter Grass novel. We kissed a small peck to each the other's lips; and then, openly smiling at one another, more like grinning, we went off on our separate ways.

"Thank you, Charles." I responded as our eyes locked for a brash second of awkward eternity. We platonically hugged. Yet, it was a beautiful, knowing hug, and for the second time in our lives we had shared ourselves, yet once again, in some vast and deeply mysterious event of spiritual oneness. I broke his embrace; our one night spent on the grassy field and this departing Vassar hug would be a fond memory of pure Poughkeepsie spontaneity.

Smiling, I made my way onto the graduation stage and found my seat. My nakedness felt like freedom under my flowing graduation gown. I picked out mom, sitting alone, in the audience. I spotted Mark a few rows behind her. He was standing and waving his arms. He looked like the scarecrow from the "Wizard of Oz." I almost burst into laughter. Then I looked back at mom, so prim in her Italian designer suit and wondered how in the hell Mark would ever fit into our billion-dollar family circle.

Mark was pointing down at his crotch. From fifty feet away I could read his lips as he mouthed out the words, "Blow me!" and I knew he was sincere, and I also knew, that he knew, that I enjoyed giving him his little masculine thrill.

I ignored him and let my eyes roam across the throng of parents and relatives of my graduating class. My guess was that there were a thousand people in the audience. And then I found myself focused on my Statistics Professor, Doctor Loomis.

He, Doc Loomis, better known as "The Loo" behind his back, was talking animatedly with Connie Becker's mother. Connie and I were roommates during our freshman year and Mrs. Becker visited our dorm often. She always brought us large bags of fresh saltwater taffy and enough dried fruits to feed the entire campus. Anyway, I watched Mom Becker walk up and kiss "The Loo" smack on his mouth.

I immediately looked around for Connie. I found her sitting three rows behind me. Our eyes met and she instantly gave me a shoulder shrug and that look of, "I have no idea as to what that's all about!" and then I knew... Rumor had it that Connie was flunking her statistics class. I looked back at her mom...

Oh boy, what was academia coming to? No pun on the word coming intended. I blocked out my thoughts and finished scanning the hoard of parents. I didn't recognize anyone else. I then found myself fixated on dad's empty chair.

A quick sadness overshadowed me. I really wanted my father to be there. This wasn't exactly high school if you know what I mean. This is Vassar. And, I am his only daughter. How could he do this to me?

A drum rolled and I watched the President and her entourage approach the stage. The ceremony was about to begin. The crowd was hushed and very little movement decried that the audience was brought to an attentive state. When the drummer's sticks went to rest, a reverent silence pervaded the entire amphitheatre. Matron Brown, a chubby French teacher, waddled up to the podium and took up the microphone.

"Ladies and gentlemen," she began as hundreds of cameras clicked back at her perfectly enunciated opening, "...we are going to be covered live by Channel 5 out of New

York City. This is a great honor to our graduating class and to the fine history of Vassar in and of herself."

Three thundering helicopters displaying the Channel 5 logo swooped gregariously down from the eastern sky to land in an empty field adjacent to the graduation arena. Camera crews and energetic Field Directors invaded the grounds like an Army platoon attacking some enemy stronghold. Within minutes of their landing, I heard a loud shout that, "Coverage is now -- LIVE!"

Ms. Brown introduced a host of Professors and finally worked her list on up to the President. The President then introduced the key guest speaker, a famous horror writer from the state of Maine, to thunderous applause, and a deafening round of student shouts. For two whole minutes the thundering of clapping hands from a standing ovation echoed about the campus.

After mentioning some of his titles, I knew immediately who this thick lens wearer was. I looked closely at him and was in such awe, a shiver ran up between my naked thighs, and I thought I'd have an orgasm, right there, on the graduate's display stage. What sheer magic he brought to this special day; and now, it was being fed live to all of New York. Oh! What a grand madness!

I noticed mom, and wondered what she was thinking. She looked distant and far off in her own private world of — who knows what? She was a Fifth Avenue shopper and her outfit for this day probably cost a 100,000 dollars.

She had boasted about her shoe store having its own zip code, and that she paid 26,000 dollars for one pair of their shoes.   Daddy approved of them. The next day, daddy gave a hospital 10 million dollars. There comes a time when I thought these were horrible excesses. I guess I still do. But the hospital gift was a nice thing.

Scanning the graduates, I discovered that I knew a few of the wealthier kids intimately. Somehow, we had gravitated together over the years. We were at ease with each other in an extremely odd way. I remembered Thad Chase, one of the super rich kids; he flew a group of us to Monaco for dinner. He lost a million dollars gambling, in about an hour. We then flew back. It was a boring trip. How crazy is that?

Donald Wicerman, we called him Don Wise-Ass, thought he could buy sex from anyone on campus. I went out with him for one whole weekend. It was fun and yeah, I gave him what he wanted. I was infatuated with him as a bright student, but his concept of love was very shallow. On the very next weekend, he asked me to join him on trip up into the Catskills, stating that he like the way I sucked his dick.

I declined, "No, Donald. You just want sex...ego sex."

Donald shrugged and walked off. Probably to delete my phone number from his cell and call someone else who was a shallow as he was. Half the girls on campus fell for his financial charm. Half of us Vassar girls, including myself, prefer the experience of mutual sex and the satisfaction of sharing pleasures. Extracurricular Sex 101 is learned outside of the classroom. It is pass/fail and Donald failed miserably with me. His pure gold Mercedes and his fat wallet full of 100 dollar bills don't impress me at all — anymore. However, I did find it exciting when he exploded in my mouth. And I thought this, with a genuine sincerity, Good luck you little prick!

And at that exact moment, as if he had heard my thought, he looked at me and smiled. It was a warped smile. A demented grin, a brash smirk, one that made me — turn my head away from him. And as I did, I came face to face with my English Professor, Doctor Evens.

Doc Evens, at forty, looked a lot younger. He could pass for one of the students and he did go to the local places where students relaxed. That's where I met him, in a nearby town called New Paltz. I was drinking Vodka Red Bulls and feeling very sexual. He told me straight up that he was a professor. But I didn't believe him. I let him hit on me thinking all the time that he was a freshman with some fun-goofy lines.

As a matter of fact, I recall telling him that I was a professor, too. I told him I was the Professor of Love or something equally as inane.

"Oh? I thought I knew most of the faculty." He seriously retorted, "Which department are you in?"

"Sociology," I lied, playfully. "I'm working on my Doctoral Thesis," I boasted. "I come here and pick up freshmen and seduce them, and if they're any good...in bed? I pull out a magic marker and give them an "A" on their penis."

"What if they aren't any good?"

"Oh. I mark a big fat "F" on their ass...in red."

As I took a sip of my drink, a group of graduate students entered and greeted Professor Eddie Evens, "Hello Doc! Hitting on the students, professor?" and, "I read your latest book, Doc, a great read!"

I made it to my 9:00 a.m. class the next morning, after teasingly placing a large red "F" on Eddie's ass. We dated secretly for two months and, I was falling in love – seriously! We met in his office often and his penis was covered with "A+" marker graffiti. And then, I overheard a bubbly-blond-bimbo telling a co-ed about all the "A's" on her professor's dick, "...as long as I pull an "A" on my finals..." and I was totally crushed, I really loved him!

I never challenged his unfaithfulness. I never told him about the conversation I overheard. I just stopped our developing relationship cold. I had Eddie for two semesters after that. It was awkward, but I received an "A" in both of his classes. And, I earned them without ever turning in a paper.

My recollection of Eddie was cut short when he seductively winked at me, and my trance was broken. I shot him the middle finger. He turned away and didn't look back. I had a brief moment of sadness as I watched him disappear... Despite everything, he was, definitely an "A+."

I saw mom again, she was on her Blackberry, but then began waving at me trying to get my attention. I waved back. She stood and yelled out something but I couldn't understand her. The President had told a joke and the audience was tattering in approval to whatever it was that she had said. I smiled at mom and made that universal hand sign that says, "Sorry! I don't know what you are saying."

Mom pointed upward. She was really enthusiastic. I hadn't seen her so animated since she played the butler a tennis match when I was ten – and won! Again, she pointed at the sky. And I read her lips, "DADDY!" and then she made herself into an airplane with extended arms. She was making a total fool of herself!

I searched the sky... I looked to where mom was pointing. Then I saw it. It was dad's helicopter. I think he has the only red one in New York. It was his, no doubt about it. Daddy was going to make it back for me after all. My heart began to race – I was so very, very happy! Everyone was standing, watching daddy land. A golf cart sped out toward the dust cloud where the whirling props continued a slow but steady spin.

Betty Parker, a genuine bitch, came up to me and asked, "That's your dad, isn't it?"

With all the pride I could muster and with all the conviction and righteousness of a pope, I emoted, "Yes. It is!"

"Well... The bastard is upstaging the entire graduation." I balled up my fist and threw a telegraphed roundhouse punch right onto her make-up laden nose. I felt the bone break and then watched her slither – unconscious – down to the stage. Blood, a lot of blood, began to ooze from her now awkwardly crooked nose. What the hell had I been thinking?

The graduation ceremony was put on pause as Betty was taken to the campus infirmary. It was an odd thing, in the hustle to help her, her grad gown fell to the side, and she was butt naked. I'm not sure what surprised me more, the fact that Betty had the balls to go naked under her gown, or that the number of volunteers increased ten-fold once her boobies were flashed!

The delay gave daddy time to join mother. They were holding hands when my name was called to go forward. I could see daddy's pride glowing ten feet around him. Mom was crying into daddy's Gucci's monogrammed handkerchief. They were the happiest couple in the audience, by far.

Unprecedented, I left the stage while they were calling the last of the names. I joined my ebullient parents in a loving huddle of milestone achievements. Mark's playful hand went up my gown as he joined in our family excitement.

"Come on, let's go celebrate."

"Okay dad, but there's a few people I have to thank first, so Mark and I will catch up with you and mom in a bit."

"That's my girl — business before pleasure!"

I had my graduation gown off before we reached my dorm room. Mark fell to his knees and magically my moistened clitoris found its way to his A+ tongue.

I bent down and whispered, "You heard my dad, business before pleasure!"

The End!

Story 5: Valentine

Chapter One

My name is Cleo Jane Starr but my friends all call me C.J., and no, Cleo is not short for Cleopatra. Although I think I am as beautiful as most Egyptian Historians have depicted her, my real claim to fame does not lie in my physical beauty but rather in my erotic views and my sense of sexual romance and the ability to pen down my sexual exploits and those of a few others.

This story is a fictional account of my closest friend and intimate, Gloria Valentine. This is her real name and I am using it here with her full permission. The fact and fiction stated here, is such that only Val herself can separate the absolute truths of this tale. I did find some of Val's statements harder to swallow than a mouth full of a Willy's warm ejaculate, but Val is quite the intricate narrator and loves emoting perceived events.

For instance, Val told me this vignette about her college Math teacher, Herman Lewis. She was failing terribly and went to discuss her fear of failing his class, and met with him, one-on-one. The old Professor was nearing seventy and had heard every excuse in the book from failing students.

"Doctor Lewis," Val began, "I'm having extreme difficulty concentrating in your class. I fixate on your crotch and fantasize on your penis. I am intrigued with wanting to know if it is still functional and whether or not you can still have orgasms."

Professor Lewis pondered her reason for failing his class and asked, "What do you propose to correct this problem, Miss Valentine? Surely, you have come here prepared to pass my course, have you not? Just what is it that you have in mind, Valentine? Perhaps you would like some tutorial assistance. That can be arranged, you know?"

"I was thinking of something that would be a whole lot simpler, Doc."

The Professor stood, showing that an erection was growing in his pants. After all, Gloria Valentine was one of the hottest chicks on campus. Lewis rounded his desk and locked his office door. Then, with a suave swagger, he approached the sitting, relaxed and grinning, failing co-ed. Now before her, he placed his hands on his own hips, and then asked her, "Would you like to earn yourself an A Miss Valentine?"

Val reached out her hands and began a slow descent of the Professor's zipper. She was surprised to find herself enjoying this old man's forward demeanor. She felt a wetness forming in her vagina and was sure as to the why. Turned on by this super erotic moment, Val loosened the bulbous head and let it extend out from the Doc's underwear and pant portal.

Lewis placed a hand behind her head and pulled her slowly forward until his penis was flush up against her lips. Then, with his left hand, he grasped his cock and guided it into her playfully teasing mouth.

Val wanted it all... Herman wanted her to take all, too! "Oh Gloria," he began moaning out his pleasure. She maneuvered his testacies out of his zipper port and into the grasp of lightly squeezing hand, With a sucking vacuum he began to throb in an uncontrolled orgasm, "Oh fuck!" came a withdrawn scream as he shot his load in a frenzy of tense spasms that sent sperm rushing explosively onto Valentine's molars.

"Don't fuck up my pants, Valentine! Swallow! OK?"

Val nodded out consent and sucked down his hot cum with a need to ingest every drop of his creative being. Val suckled on until the saline tasting juice was no longer oozing from the tiny hole at the center of his penis's head. With a thumb and index finger, she tried to force out another taste, another drop of the professorial sperm.

Val wanted orgasm from clitoral touch. Never mind that it was not her teacher's fingers that brought her to orgasm, but her own hand of delight and a rapid flay of dexterous play, "Oh My God!" reverberated down the outside hallway and was heard by at least a dozen turned-curious coeds.

***

Val laughs continuously when she tells this story and I have never heard her say it the same way twice. This is now the official first story of, Valentine. I will be back soon with more stories of my friend Val, and I may even tell you one that is just about me, C.J. Starr.

About the Author

C. J. Starr is the author of the bestselling City Girl Series. These Quickie Stories are about women with high ambition and libido to match. These steam reads are filled with humor, romance, and of course, lots of sex!

A Special Note from C. J.

Thank you so much for reading my stories! I hope you enjoyed these quickie reads as much as I did. Sex is the best, now go get a good rest and prepare yourself to read more of my delicious stories. Hey, visit my website too at CJStarr.net.

xoxo, C. J. Starr

Quickie Reads by C. J. Starr

www.ingramcontent.com/pod-product-compliance
Lightning Source LLC
Chambersburg PA
CBHW071131250626
47159CB00006B/2196